Weekly Reader Children's Book Club presents

What Kind of Bird is That?

By Mirra Ginsburg
Pictures by Giulio Maestro

Adapted from a Russian story by V. Suteyev

Crown Publishers, Inc. New York

Text copyright © 1973 by Mirra Ginsburg
Illustrations copyright © 1973 by Giulio Maestro
All rights reserved. No part of this publication may be reproduced,
stored in a retrieval system, or transmitted, in any form or by any means,
electronic, mechanical, photocopying, recording, or otherwise,
without the prior written permission of the Publisher.
Inquiries should be addressed to Crown Publishers, Inc.,
419 Park Avenue South, New York, N.Y. 10016.
Printed in the United States of America
Library of Congress Catalog Card Number: 72-91703
ISBN: 0-517-50255-0
Published simultaneously in Canada by General Publishing Company Limited
First Printing

The text of this book is set in 18 pt. Bookman.
The illustrations are pen and ink drawings reproduced in halftone,
with three additional flat colors.
Weekly Reader Children's Book Club Edition

For
Norma Jean

Once upon a time there lived a Goose.
He envied everybody and was always
quarreling and hissing: "S-s-s! S-s-s!"

All the other birds and animals
and people shook their heads and said,
"My, what a very silly goose."

One day the Goose saw a Swan on
the lake. He liked the Swan's long neck.
"If only I could have a neck like that!"
he thought.
"Let us trade," he said to the Swan.
"I'll give you my neck, if you will
give me yours."

The Swan thought it over and agreed.

The Goose walked on with the long
swan neck and did not know what to do
with it.

He turned it,

he stretched it,

he rolled it up
like a wheel,

but no matter what he did
he was not comfortable.

"You are neither goose nor swan! Ha-ha-ha!"
laughed a Pelican.
The Goose was insulted and wanted to hiss,
but suddenly he noticed the Pelican's
beak with the large sack under it.

"Ah, if only I could have such a beak,"
  thought the Goose.
"Let us trade," he said to the Pelican.
"I'll give you my beak if you will
  give me yours."

The Pelican laughed and agreed.

"How clever I am," thought the Goose. "Now I can get everything I want by trading, and I will become the finest goose in the world."

He traded legs with the Crane. In exchange
for his short legs with their flat webbed
feet, he got the Crane's long, elegant legs.

He traded his large white wings for
the Crow's little black wings.

Then he saw a Peacock, opening and closing his great shimmering tail. It took the Goose a long time to convince the Peacock to trade it for his own short one which could only waggle from side to side. But the Peacock finally got tired of the Goose and traded with him.

When the Goose had nothing more to trade, the kindhearted Rooster simply gave him his comb, his wattle, and even his loud ringing "Cock-a-doodle-do."

Now the Goose looked like no other bird in
the world. He strode on the Crane's long legs,
proudly waving the great peacock tail
and turning the long swan neck this way
and that, until he met a flock of geese.

"Ga-ga-ga! What kind of bird is that?"
wondered the geese.
"I am a goose!" cried the Goose. He flapped
the Crow's wings, stretched the Swan's neck,
and sang out with the Pelican's huge beak:
"Cock-a-doodle-do! I am the most beautiful
goose on earth!"

"Well, if you are a goose, come with us,"
said the geese.

They came to a field.

All the geese plucked the fresh sweet
grass, but the Goose could only clack
his enormous beak with its sack.
The beak was made for catching fish, and
the Goose could not pluck a single
blade of grass with it.

Then the geese went to the lake to swim, and the Goose went with them. They swam merrily, but the Goose could only run back and forth along the bank. The Crane's long legs were made for wading, not for swimming. "Ga-ga-ga!" laughed the geese.

"Cock-a-doodle-do!" answered the Goose.

The geese came out of the water.
Suddenly a fox jumped out of the reeds.
The geese spread their wings and rose
into the air.

Only the Goose remained. The Crow's
little wings could not lift him up.
He started running on the Crane's legs,
but the Peacock's splendid tail got
tangled in the reeds.

The Fox caught him by the Swan's long neck.
But the geese came flying from all
directions, beating the Fox with their
wings and pecking him with their beaks.

The Fox let the Goose go and ran for dear life.
"Thank you for saving me," said the Goose.
"Now I know what I must do."

He went to the Swan and gave him his long, lovely neck.

He returned the large beak with its sack
to the Pelican, the long, slender legs
to the Crane,

the little black wings to the Crow,

the bright, fanlike tail to the Peacock,
and the comb, the wattle, and the
"Cock-a-doodle-do" to the kind Rooster.

He became a goose like all other geese,
but now he was wise and kind and never
envied anyone again.

And that is the end of the story
about the Goose.